D1577671

For my parents

Random House Australia Pty Ltd
20 Alfred Street, Milsons Point, NSW 2061

Sydney New York Toronto
London Auckland Johannesburg
and agencies throughout the world

First published in 1988 by Walker Books Ltd
87 Vauxhall Walk, London SE11 5HJ

First published in Australia in 1994

ISBN 0-09-183003-6

Printed in Italy

Dear Wally
Happy Birthday
love (Good on ya!)
4.1.96

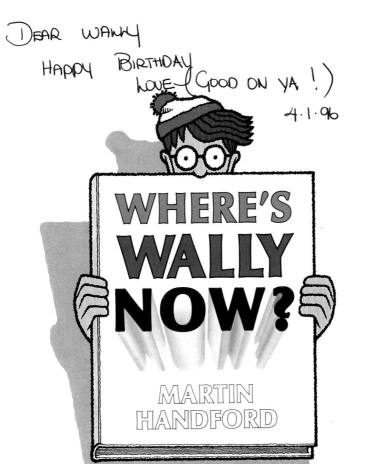

WHERE'S WALLY NOW?

MARTIN HANDFORD

RANDOM HOUSE

AUSTRALIA

THE ABSOLUTELY HUGE AND ENORMOUSLY INTERESTING BOOK OF CAVEMEN, CAVE WOMEN, CAVE DOGS AND ALL SORTS OF EXTREMELY SAVAGE STONE-AGE BEASTS.

HI THERE, BOOK WORMS! WELL I'LL TELL YOU THIS FOR NOTHING – SOME BITS OF HISTORY ARE GREAT, FANTASTIC, JUST AMAZING! I SIT HERE READING ALL THESE BOOKS ABOUT THE WORLD LONG AGO, AND IT'S LIKE RIDING A TIME-MACHINE. WITH A LITTLE IMAGINATION I CAN REALLY GO PLACES, WOW! PHEW! IT'S WILD! WHY NOT TRY IT FOR YOURSELVES, WALLY FOLLOWERS? JUST SEARCH EACH PICTURE AND FIND ME, WOOF (REMEMBER, ALL YOU CAN SEE IS HIS TAIL), WENDA, WIZARD WHITEBEARD AND ODLAW. AND ONE MORE THING! CAN YOU FIND ANOTHER CHARACTER, NOT SHOWN BELOW, WHO APPEARS ONCE IN EVERY PICTURE? COME ON AND FOLLOW US THROUGH TIME!

Wally

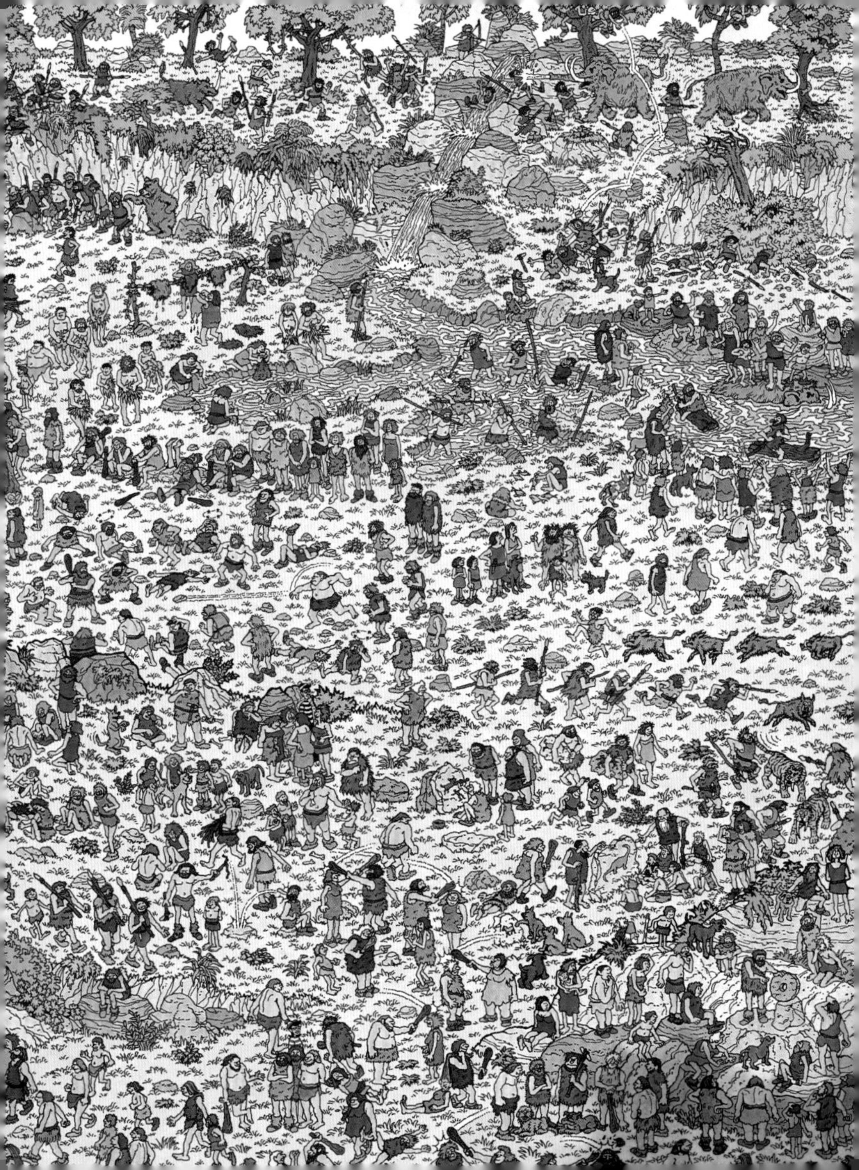

THE RIDDLE OF THE PYRAMIDS

The ancient Egyptians were very clever people who loved goats, cats and sphinx, and invented pyramids. With great difficulty they built several huge pyramids in the desert. But now no one can remember why. Were they adventure playgrounds for Egyptian mummies and babies, or were they houses without any of the useful bits?

Is it possible (or even likely) that pharaohs were buried under them? These questions are as hard to answer as a camel's hump.

FUN AND GAMES
IN
ANCIENT ROME

The Romans spent most of their time fighting, conquering, learning Latin and making roads. When they took their holidays, they always had games at the Coliseum (an old sort of playground). Their favourite games were fighting, more fighting, chariot racing, fighting and feeding Christians to lions. When the crowd gave a gladiator the thumbs down, it meant kill your opponent. Thumbs up meant let him go, to fight to the death another day.

1,003 YEARS AGO

ON TOUR
WITH THE
VIKINGS

At home the Vikings were quiet
people who liked knitting and cheese
tasting and boring things like that.
But on tour they went wild. They
put on their best horned hats and
sailed across the sea, singing and
shouting like mad. If you heard them
coming, it was best to run away,
because once they had arrived and
unpacked their axes, there was no
holding them back.

THE END OF THE CRUSADES

800 YEARS AGO

After 200 years of fierce argument with the Saladins and Paladins, who would not tell them the way to Jerusalem, the Crusaders finally ran out of clean T-shirts, so they came home. For years afterwards they dined out on stories of the lovely castles they had battered and besieged and the fascinating people they had thrown rocks at, so the Crusades were not a complete waste of time after all.

ONCE UPON A SATURDAY MORNING

The Middle Ages were a very merry time to be alive, especially on Saturdays, as long as you didn't get caught. Short skirts and stripy tights were in fashion for men; everybody knew lots of jokes; there was widespread juggling and jousting and archery and jesting and fun. But if you got into trouble, the Middle Ages could be miserable. For the man in the stocks or the pillory or about to lose his head, Saturday morning was no laughing matter.

THE LAST DAYS OF THE AZTECS

The Aztecs lived in sunny Mexico and were rich and strong and liked swinging from poles pretending to be eagles. They also liked making human sacrifices to their gods, so it was best to agree with everything they said. The Spanish were also rich and strong, and some of them, called conquistadors, came to Mexico in 1519 to have an adventure. They thought the Aztecs were a complete nuisance, only good for arguing with and fighting.

400 YEARS AGO

Is red better than blue? What do you mean your poem about cherry blossom is better than mine? Shall we have another cup of tea? Over difficult questions such as these, the Japanese fought fiercely for hundreds of years. The fiercest fighters of all were the samurai, who wore flags on their backs so that their mummies could find them. The fighters without flags were called ashigaru. They couldn't take a joke any better than the samurai, especially about their hair.

TROUBLE IN OLD JAPAN

BEING A PIRATE

(Shiver-me-timbers!)

It was really a lot of fun being a pirate, especially if you were very hairy and didn't have much in the way of brains. It also helped if you only had one leg, or one eye, or two noses, and had a pirate's hat with your name-tag sewn inside and a treasure-map and a rusty cutlass. Once there were lots of pirates, but they died out in the end because too many of them were men (which is not a good idea).

HAVING A BALL IN GAYE PAREE

The history of France has some very bad bits, like geting your head chopped off by Madame Guillotine in the French Revolution; and some very good bits, like the invention of smelly cheese. In 1870 Napoleon (the third one) threw a marvellous ball in Paris to celebrate 1870 being a good bit. All the beautiful people came and danced the night away to a band called the Third Republic.

THE
GOLD

RUSH

At the end of the nineteenth century large numbers of excited Americans were frequently to be seen rushing headlong towards holes in the ground, hoping to find gold. Most of them never even found the holes in the ground. But at least they all had a good day, with plenty of exercise and fresh air, which kept them healthy. And health is much more valuable than gold ... well, nearly more valuable ... isn't it?

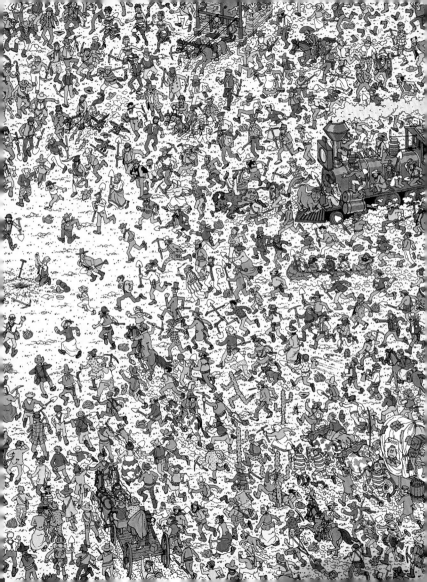